"The money we raise will pay for a new roof."
Everybody has to bring something to sell.

"Why don't you give your old jack-in-the-box, Peppa?"
suggests Daddy Pig.

"Oh, OK," agrees Peppa. "Now it's
your turn, Daddy. What are you going
to give?"

Daddy Pig is not sure.
"What about your squeaky old chair?"
suggests Peppa helpfully.

"But it's very old and valuable," says
Daddy Pig.
"Hee! Hee!" says Mummy Pig. "You
found it on a rubbish tip!"

When Madame Gazelle arrives in her truck, Mummy Pig, Peppa and George give her everything to take to the jumble sale.

Naughty Mummy Pig gives her Daddy
Pig's squeaky chair, too.
"Daddy Pig will never notice," she
whispers to Peppa.

It is the day of the jumble sale.
There are lots of things to buy.

Mummy Pig wants to buy some fruit
and vegetables.
Daddy Pig wants to buy a chocolate cake.

"Peppa," says Miss Rabbit. "How about buying this chair? You can chop it up and use it for firewood."

"But Daddy says it's very old and worth lots of money!" says Peppa.

All Peppa's friends have given
something to the jumble sale.
Suzy has given her nurse's outfit.

Pedro has given his balloon, Danny Dog has given his car and Candy Cat has given her skipping rope.

"I will miss my jack-in-the-box,"
sighs Peppa.
"I will miss playing at nurses," says
Suzy sadly.
Peppa's friends all think they will
miss their toys, so they buy them
back again.

"Look what I've bought!" snorts Daddy
Pig. "It's an antique chair to match my
old one!"
"Oh, Daddy!" Mummy Pig laughs.
"It matches your old one because it IS
your old one!" snorts Peppa.

"But Miss Rabbit has just charged
me lots of money for it!" says poor
Daddy Pig.
"Fantastic news!" says Madame
Gazelle.

"We have just raised all the money
we need for a new school roof!"
"Hooray!" everybody cheers.